EXCALIBRE

CONSTANTINE O'DONNELL

ISBN: 978-1-63950-241-7 (sc)
ISBN: 978-1-63950-242-4 (e)

Writers Apex

Gateway Towards Success

8063 MADISON AVE #1252
Indianapolis, IN 46227
+13176596889
www.writersapex.com

This book is dedicated to my Auntie Sheila O'Donnell aka Dickson. She lives in Scotland where my Granny O'Donnell aka Ward came from. I want to tell you that Auntie Sheila thought my little brother was the Boss when my Daddy died because he left my little brother the O'Donnell land…a 30 acre farm…pretty good, eh?! My brother is a good young man…he is a genius as well. I am the biggest genius in the family but because of my terrible upbringing lol just playing about…because of my bad behaviour when I was young and drinking and doing drugs my Daddy left the farm to my little brother. I was quite dismayed but I got over it. My Auntie Sheila said to my brother while I was within earshot "You're the boss now…" My father had just died. I was extremely annoyed by this…my brother was extremely happy. I do not care who is the boss but it was a bit of a kick in the teeth for me. I am the Boss of my family now that my Dad died in a fatal blowjob lol just kidding…a blowjob is where the woman sucks the mans penis…you'll learn all about it when you're older…maybe sooner if you are lucky lol…if you give a man a blowjob remember to swallow the sperm…it is the best feeling for the man you are giving the blowjob to…it is warm and salty…but do not spit it out…it ruins the mood of sexual pleasure…my Daddy died because his heart gave in…I wasn't sad because he was so bad to me when I got diagnosed mentally ill. I will explain how that came about in this book…I'll break it down for you so it won't be that complicated…anyway my Auntie Sheila agrees that I am now the Boss of the O'Donnell Royal Family.

The book you are about to read little ones is about your King Constantine O'Donnell.

Here are the factors with which he lives under.

He is an Ultragenius. He is Psychic. That means he can hear your thoughts.

The mass media i.e. newspapers and television are ruining his name. They are not mentioning him in the papers but they are talking about him on the television. He can hear them through the wall in his sitting room. He doesn't have a television but the wicked old battle axe next door puts hers up full blast. She is evil. Evil exists in the world but as aliens of Pachsion, we are going to stamp it out. Do not be afraid. God does not exist. We invented him. We needed to give the human race something to believe in. If they knew there was aliens, there would have been no work done. People would have sat back waiting on our intervention. The God scenario meant that we could control the Earthlings that believed in him and make Earth a nice place to live. There are many religions but Catholicism is our religion. The rest were made up by Earthlings. If you believe in Jesus, then you are a good person. He was being told what to do by aliens as well. Just like your King, Con…aka Constantine.

The last thing Con wants is to be killed by humans for telling them that God doesn't exist but he is not afraid to die. Either should you be. When you die, you come to Pachsion. Our homeworld. 100 billion light years away…very far away!!!

The only life that will exist on Earth if Con dies will be the cockroaches…
just like a nuclear explosion. They will be the building blocks of a new
humanity.

The only real reason humans such as Psychiatrists want Con dead is
because he knows mental health does not exist. It is all in human's
minds. They must help themselves. The only existence that Con will
experience when he dies will be eternal happiness. That is what you will
experience as well. So, when you are told to got to bed, do not argue!

All children of the ages 5 and up will be sexually active. They will
be allowed to experiment with each other. It is terrible that sex is
kept so secret by adults. That is why so many children do not have
a good sex life when they get older. They have been smothered with
terrible parenting. As your leader, Con will teach you in his book iCon
wildman101. You can read it when you are 13. All boys and girls will be
allowed to read it in their school and will have homework assignments
on it.

The only thing that really annoys Con is people telling lies about him.
He is a very well-rounded individual. He is a world traveller. He is a
Sailor. They have lots of fun.

I am Con's guide on Earth. I talk to him in his mind. He hears my voice
all day every day and at night in his dreams. I look out for him. I am
on Pachsion. I do not sleep ever. The world I live in has 3 sun's and a
transparent atmosphere. There are stars in the sky 24 hours a day. It is
beautiful. You will see it when you come here. If you are a good person.
Do not be evil. You will not be welcome.

I as King, am going to have a breather now…this little book I am
writing really excites me. My children will be reading it in a few years
time. I am going to have many children.

Andrea Garbula aka Bombardier will be the best mother in the world. All moms will be admiring her. She is the coolest woman I have ever met.

The aliens are going to be the only guidance for your young lives. You will not watch television anymore. All the internet will be open to you but you will not sit and vegetate in front of a television. You will read books…all of the Famous Five and Magnificent seven…anything by Enid Blyton. JK Rowling as well. That should keep you going for a few years until you are old enough to read my autobiography iCon wildman101 and my poetry book Anonymous in the Town that Talks and The Giant's Causeway.

If you would like to learn how to write poetry like an alien just write the first line…then the second line…then the third line and make the last word in the second line rhyme with the last word in the fourth line… it is easy when you expand your vocabulary…read the dictionary. Ask your parents to buy you a little dictionary and sit and look up words… learn them off and their meanings. If you really like writing poetry ask your parents to buy you a Rhyming dictionary. It is all the words that rhyme with one another. John Shanty from The Sean ti bar in Greencastle told me about it. I'd never heard of it…it is really easy to write songs and poetry when you use it. It will inspire you!

I am going to get some beer and cigarettes now…you're too young to drink and smoke. You need to be 12…not going yet. My driver is busy…he is a workaholic and he is 77 lol he's only 75…you'll not be working at that age. You will be retired at 45…the same age I retired at. You will all be wealthy. The aliens are giving everybody in the world 5 million dollars when they reach 45. You will work as normal up until that at whatever profession…job…you want to work at…I have time to show you how to write poetry like the aliens…here is a sample…

I am an author,

Of so much infamy,

The police fucking hate me,

They want be to be a dummy,

Sucking on the social services,

Drawing the dole,

Crawling home,

After a night of cajole,

By the bar staff,

Who are always on my hole…

Well dear children,

That isn't how,

I planned my life,

I am King Con now!!!

The lovely people who talk about my book iCon wildman101 are the salt of the Earth…I do not mean poor but genuine…you will all be salt of the Earth if you follow my instructions on how to live your lives. Do not worry…I am not your Daddy…he will educate you as well…so will your mother…they will read extensively as well. Television will become a thing of the past. Watching mind numbing programming for hours on end…not using your grey matter i.e. your brain…'i.e.' means 'That is…'. Your parents are already good people for letting you read this book. They have evolved and they will guide you on your way through life. Do not let them be nasty to you. Do not sulk if they are wrong… tell them to not be so bad to you or you will tell me!!! The aliens will be talking to you in your minds. You have an inner voice advising you on everything. The voice you hear comes from Pachsion…our home planet…100 billion light years away…you are psychic…all humans are psychic…the world did not know that until this very moment. Do you feel privileged knowing this? Privileged means special.

Everybody with a talent will be shot into fame…everybody has special gifts in this world…we give you them in the womb…we are the controllers of Earth. Earth is about to be a holiday destination for the rest of the Universe. That is why Earth was created. Earth is only a few thousand years old. There is no Santa Claus or God, angels, demons or the Devil. We created all that to give a sense of mysticism to the planet. Just look what we've inspired on Earth…movies, books and spiritual beings roaming the Earth. There are ghosts on Earth but they do not have a host anymore…they will talk to you but they will not inhabit you. You are quite safe and sound!

Mental illness is something you will hear about. It was the scourge of the planet before your King…me…put himself in harms way and signed himself in to a mental asylum to combat the poor treatment of patients by vicious psychiatric nurses and psychiatrists. The whole thing is controlled by a big corporation called Pharmaceuticals. They are not going to be giving anybody psychotropic medication ever again when I, the Alien King, vanquish them!!!

The only people that will help you if you have psychological problems will be counsellors. There will be millions of brilliant counsellors in the world…I am going to be paying them myself and the job will be very well paid…maybe you should be a counsellor…you obviously have a very bright mind if you are reading this!!! I will hire you and pay you millions to help the world…

The world is a playground…I love living here…but my homeworld according to my alien guide, Sachsion, is unbelievable…you will be coming to it when you die in many years from now…you will have all your memories of your life on Earth so make them good ones. Travel the world when you are young…make love…that means have sex with lots of men and women…humans are bisexual…that means you get turned on i.e. aroused sexually, by both men and women.

The last thing you should be is a tell tale…my father told me when I was young and came home from school and started telling him about what happened at school…he said sternly…that means kind of crossly…"No tales out of school!!!" That was a lesson to me. He was a great mentor when I was young. I carried this ethos…ethos means feeling…into my adulthood and never told tales on anybody. You will not be bad mouthed by anybody…bad mouthed means talked badly about…if you keep your mouth shut…it is called Omerta.

I am the King of the I.R.A.…the British media call me a terrorist…I am a Freedom Fighter. I have never killed anybody but that doesn't mean I wouldn't if my life is in perilous danger…you should be the same!

I am a gifted writer and singer…and believe it or not dancer as well. My dancing is very influenced by my martial arts upbringing. If you want to feel secure travelling the world then learn Krav Maga. It is the best martial arts on the planet. If you want to be really good at Krav maga then learn as many other martial arts as you can. You will pick up moves that will always be in you weapon armoury…that means you will be very good at defending yourself forever. I was a Karate expert at 9 years of age. My kicking was supreme. I once scored over the limit in a fight one time because I won so many points so fast in the fight lol. The club wanted me then to fight the under 14 Ulster Champion when I was 9 years old. I scored a point off him and he got so angry that he kicked me in the stomach with a roundhouse kick…you'll learn what that is when you're doing your Karate…the kick left me winded…that means knocked all the air out of my lungs making it really painful to breath…I began crying. The crowd booed. He was dishonoured. My Dad was Sensei and he picked me up onto my feet and told me I was just winded and I'd be fine…stop your crying he said…toughen up! I stopped crying and got the respect from both teams.

My father was a cool Sensei. He did not put up with any shit…that means if you misbehaved he'd kick your ass. He once got rid of an asshole in the class by standing on his big toe just to anger him. He pressed down on the bully's toe so the bully would react. The bully screamed "Get off my bleedin' toe you idiot…" My father said "You are out of here for dissent…now get the fuck out…and don't come back!!!" The bully yelled at him "I'm telling my father on you…" My dad said "Go tell him…I'll do the same to him…" That was the end of the bully in the class. Everybody else learned a lesson as well…including me. I was only 7. I have never bullied anybody in my life, even when I was young. I might make fun of people but only as a joke and not if it hurts them.

The Karate we were learning is called Wado ryu. It comes from China. I learned it in Derry…Londonderry for the British…soon to be Derry forever…the city of London in England will be called Londonderry. It is pretty good for having a fight but wrestling is better for fighting in the playground at school. Karate is too violent. You will get into trouble. I was always in trouble with our Head Master Tom dickhead Harkin…just kidding. I don't hold any grudges but he always singled me out because I knew Karate and used it on anybody who picked a fight with me as a kid. I was kickass!!! At least with wrestling you can get your bully to submit without really injuring him. It will be enough to tell him to fuck right off!!!

Darwin's theory of evolution is complete crap. We put life on Earth. Us the aliens!!!

If your parents think you are too rowdy and want to put you on psychotropic medication refuse it. You are a child…you are always going to be rowdy until you mature…that means get wise.

The aliens are laughing at Con...me...they realise I just want to get drunk today and not bother writing anything lol Con is the ultimate party animal...you will all be the same.

The parents that let their children read this book are so evolved... we know they are out there...we have inspired them to let their kids like you read this. You are a little adult...not like Scientology...that is a made up religion...not like Catholicism where we made it up lol... Scientology tries to make children adults by talking to them in an adult fashion...that just makes you lose your childhood...we are going to eradicate all religion...there is no God like we told you. There is only aliens and we control the Earth. Con is the main man...me.

The reason I call this book The Getaway Clause is because you will be leaving home at 15 years old and starting your journey on Earth as an adult. The new life plan for the human race is to be mature enough at that age to be able to sustain yourself without your parents interfering. The parents who still interfere will be put in prison lol just kidding... they will be told leave your kids alone!!!

I am the King of the Universe...I know how to rule people. I rule the world Pachsion from Earth...my RaCons...my underground army in the Universe...are updating me every so often with reports of how my actions are affecting the planet Earth. The last time they told me that I was being killed by my own people...the I.R.A...they are the Irish Republican Army...they fought the british for over a century to bring a United Ireland...google The Troubles in Northern Ireland...you will see the fight that they, we, had. The I.R.A did not like me taking over their little country...they just deal drugs now illegally. That is all they do. They are Criminals but that is what they had to be to bring guns and bomb material into the country under the law's noses lol. The aliens did not allow anything to happen me. They stopped them in their tracks. The U.V.F are now threatening me as well...they are not of the same calibre of terrorists…freedom fighters they are not…the are a reactionary group set up to fight the I.R.A as part of a government ploy. They will be quashed as well by the aliens. The aliens tell them in their thoughts when they decide to kill me that they will all get Leukaemia… the aliens are serious. The u.v.f are called the ulster freedom fighters as well. They are not fighting for any freedom…they only resort to thuggery…and killing of innocent people. The I.R.A always attacked political targets. They did not mean to kill innocent people during their campaign of War against the british. The british are from another planet. They are from britannia. It is the closest planet to Pachsion. They did not want to be ruled by anybody else in the Universe. They wanted to rule themselves but we want peace throughout the Universe and they are not a peaceful planet…so many deaths every day through war on their planet. We stepped in and told them that they need to calm down so all the planets in the Universe got together and had a meeting. The Kings of each planet decided the best course of action was to start a new planet with people from every planet in the Universe…hundreds of them…and see who rises to the top? They invented Earth…we are the most advanced planet so the job of creating it was up to us…not a bad job, eh?! The Pachsion King agreed to this and picked Ireland as the country for the Pachsion people. The britannia King said we will live beside you on britain and see if we can cohabit…that means live peacefully together…they could not do it and invaded many times over the millenia. They could not take Pachsion being so productive and peaceful…within reason lol…us Celtic Warriors have a serious temper so there were many inhouse wars but the people were in general very happy. The britannia people could not take this and tried to take over Ireland so many times in it's history…they tried to reason with the Irish…Pachsion…but the Irish would not hear tell of britain ruling Ireland. The british people are very arrogant in their attitude. They think they are superior to the rest of the Universe…the british people have descended from britannia and the attitude came down through their ancestry…just like Craicealte or Craic…this means crazy in Irish Gaelic…our language on Pachsion…came down through our ancestry. We are the funnest aliens in the Universe and the most peaceful until annoyed…this is obvious in our fight back against the british. Your King Con was raised an Assassin for the I.R.A but he never did a killing mission. He was Top Brass and the dirty work like killing people is left to the underlings…they have no life plan like our King Con… Con is the King of the I.R.A on Earth and the Universe. The U.V.F and U.D.A…Ulster death assholes lol something like that!!!…are the protestant…google protestant…fighting force on Ireland. They see themselves as british but they are in fact naturalised English into Irish society. That means they are welcome here but they must realise this is not their country!!! And never was…that is the end to the Dirty War in Ireland. Con is marrying a Queen from Canada called Andrea Garbula. She is a flaming red head and is absolutely stunning. He has done very well for himself lol she was handpicked by his wife on Pachsion to be his soulmate on Earth. That woman has saved his life! He thought he would never meet an equal but he has met the Granddaughter of a genius Engineer and inventor called…this excites Con when he sees the word inventor…he loves inventions because he is an Engineer as well… his favourite subject at school…Bombardier…the family are thee most wealthy Canadians and the most fun family you could ever meet… Con only knows this because Drea (Andrea calls herself this…I think it suits her dark side…all Con's women thru his life have been dark… femme fatales…google that…) told him her family love to get their drink on!!! The threat from the paramilitaries…this means terrorists… is going to stop very soon…it will stop as soon as this book hits the world stage…Con is getting married in Westminster Abbey in London, uk. This is monumental! The british people will all be angry and they will not want an I.R.A man to be King of Britain as well as the rest of the world but my dear children the King of Britannia handed over to him last night…he came to Con psychically and told him "You rule us too now…" So British people the homeworld you come from has been beaten by the I.R.A…the Pachsion Freedom Fighters…the u.v.f and u.f.f and u.d.a and any other godamned fucking asshole regiment of the British Army orange idiots that are angry at the loss must now come to terms with it and allow themselves to live in Ireland alongside the Catholic…the Catholic religion is the Pachsion invented religion… all religions were invented by us…they all came from King Con…even the Jewish lol…Muslim is so antiquated and must stop immediately… it is so unbelievably controlling…people. They will be allowed to live on this little island as long as they behave themselves…if they don't they will go to prison in Australia…we won't go into what the prison is like…you're a bit too young…we don't want you to have nightmares and wet your little bed lol…you can read about it in The Giant's Causeway when you are 12…the rest of humanity is made up of other ridiculous beliefs…they are outrageously funny…the Indian people praying to a cow and a god with a dozen arms is so funny…you will laugh at the evolution of Earth when you study it at school in our new schooling system in a few short years time…all of Earths history…so colourful… will be taught to you. It will be the same teachings in every school on the planet. The Earth will be such a fun place for you to grow up in now!!!

The last thing Con is going to write today is his favourite…a little poem…it's about the I.R.A beating the U.V.F…

UV Rays

The U.V.F are a bunch of thugs,
They had the Shankill butchers,
Con gave them a rub,
He was on the beer in Belfast,
And was guided to the Shankill road,

He walked into the pub The Crown,

And said jokingly "GOD SAVE THE QUEEN!!!",

This was met,

With raised fucking eyebrows,

The barman did not know,

What to do,

Con had a pint,

And left the bar,

He marched down the Shankill,

On his own,

He was muttering Up the Celtic,

And the Chinese wall,

He is a world ruler,

These thugs were always going to fall!!!

Tiocfaidh ar la!!!

The next thing I am going to tell you kids is about the Jews…they come from an evil planet called Zion…they created their own religion on earth so they would feel special…they were not given a country because they are the most devious people in the Universe…they have been responsible for so much pain and suffering on earth. We picked one of them to be a sacrifice and create Catholicism…his name was Jesus. You will have heard of him being crucified on the a cross and killed. The Roman empire did this to him because he was causing unrest among their subjects…subjects are people who are under rule. The Roman Emperor Constantine was so affected by Jesus that he converted to Catholicism on his death bed. The rest of the Romans converted too and that is why it is called Roman Catholic!

The Jewish people are a vile product of their homeworld Zion… they are now trying to take over my country Ireland…they are using pharmaceutical money to try and bring peace to our land…they used my army the I.R.A to do this. They gave them lots of money and told

them they would be killed by a superior being if they did not comply...
comply means agree. The head honcho...honcho means boss...is a
Real I.R.A man. This term for the I.R.A was invented by the Jews
as a manipulation technique to scare people...like we said they are
extremely evil.

The British government know the plan of the Jews...they allow the
Real I.R.A to exist.

The Pachsion people who are the REAL IRISH REPUBLICAN
ARMY have not cottoned on to the plan yet...they are all too busy
with the peace process thinking that the whole thing can be solved
by inept...inept means useless...politicians. The leader of the I.R.A
Politicians is a hero called Gerry Adams. He was very influential in my
life but his writing is boring as sin lol!!!

The I.R.A are going to come together and get rid of the Real I.R.A.
The Real I.R.A are a bunch of halfwits who are living off the glory of
the legitimate I.R.A...I hope this is not too complicated for you but if
you read it carefully and think about it, you will understand it.

The Zionist people...the Jews...are going to be eradicated lol just
their theory on how life on earth should be lived. They are a very
neurotic people...so paranoid...it is because they think everybody
is as evil as them. They invented a word for abuse of them...such is
their manipulation of the human race!!! Fucking Jewish backstabbing
cunts lol hope they're not reading this or they will complain to their
psychiatrist that they are being victimised lol...they will cry and say
that I am being anti-semitic...that is a bloody good term in my book!!!
Google anti-semitic to you see the manipulation they put up on the
internet...do not believe a word of it...we are ethnically cleansing
them like our Hero Adolf Hitler...we told Adolf to do what he did...
we experimented on them to find out what made them so evil...we

wanted them to be at peace with themselves and thought we could do this by teaching them a lesson…Adolf Hitler is a Hero to millions and millions of people who have had Real life experience of a Jew…the only good thing they created was my favourite fighting self defence martial arts…Krav Maga…YouTube Bruce Lee of Krav Maga and you will meet my new Sensei…I am going to get him to bring me up the level of proficiency in it…proficiency means expert!

The Zion people are being obliterated for disobeying the treaty… treaty means agreement…this is all lawyer talk…don't worry you will get used to it!

Zion people will no longer exist in the Universe. All the other planets are in agreement with Con that they must be killed to eradicate evil in the Universe…Con was at the brunt end of their treatment and massive manipulation…that's what the psychiatrists are trained in… stay fucking away from those cocksuckers!!!

I am going to take a break for a cigarette now and cough violently and hear messages from the other Universe that created everything… where they came from is still a secret…I'm sure you're wondering where everything originated…as Con calls it…the index human…who was the first?…we can tell you now his name was Donnell…his children were all given his name as their surname…if you know anything about the Irish Pachsion people…O MEANS GRANDSON OF…MEANING YOU WILL HAVE THE TRAITS OF YOUR GRANDFATHER… MC MEANS THE SON OF…MEANING YOU WILL HAVE THE TRAITS OF YOUR FATHER…O IS THE SUPERIOR RACE IN PACHSION…traits means to have similar personalities.

I am the only person I know who has never been beaten in a fight!!!

When I was young, I was always fighting with the bully's…I always beat them eventually…even if it was 40 years later…I always got them back…they will never bully me again!!!

Street fighting is very dangerous…anything could happen…there are knives and broken bottles involved and sometimes guns as well…you can get seriously hurt or killed so only do it if your life depends upon it…learn Krav Maga!!!

Karate is brilliant for toughness and kicking…you learn lots of cool punches as well like the one my father taught a solicitor pupil of his in front of me after class…it was blackbelt level…I was watching him teach Donal McGuinness…Daddy's favourite pupil…how to do it into the kick pad…that's how powerful it is…we are going to have a complete world governing body of martial arts…everything will be combined and you will learn the most proficient of all these moves!!!

Con learned all the moves he knows from attending classes through his life…as the new age kids call it because of video games…he has lots of moves from all the martial arts he learned from all the different styles in his armoury…HE IS THE ULTIMATE WARRIOR!!!

The Jewish people will forgive my anti semitic comments when they realise I am not going to eradicate them off earth…they are going to be receiving their dream of owning a country for creating Krav Maga and helping the human race to defend themselves should the need arise… their country will be Zaire in Africa…it'll be fun watching their pasty complexion turn brown as a berry lol…they will call Zaire…Zion. The promised land!!!

All Jews on earth will be coming to Pachsion when they die…as long as they behave themselves!!!

My Daddy told me "From little acorns, big trees grow…" This means even the smallest of ideas can grow into massive results…he inspired me so much…pity he was so controlling and sided with the Jews when I was 25…you will read about that in my autobiography 'Shroove Head' in the coming year!!!

The Jewish people have lots of jokes about them on Pachsion…here is one of them…what do you call a Jew in a barber shop?...a fucking cleaner…ever see their beards lol?

The Zionist people of Zion on earth will be the most happiest people in Africa…they will have Zillions of dollars and a carte blanche…that means a clean sheet…to build their dream country!

The Pachsion people will be the peace keepers of the Universe. They will have the only guns in the Universe.

The British King Charles will relinquish his Kingship to the Irish King Constantine…Tiocfaidh ar la!!!

This will happen live on television and online when he marry's Andrea the Queen of Canada…King Charles will place his crown on Con's head after the priest has finished the ceremony…Prince Harry will be one of Con's groomsmen. He always liked him in the media and really enjoyed his book 'SPARE'…only the one of a few books that Con has read in a couple of days…so interesting…Con loved his mother Lady Diana…he was really upset when she died…even as an I.R.A King!

The British government are going to be so bloody proud of their Royal family for bowing down to the Irish Royal Family lol they will want to go to war…that is why they are being disbanded!!!

The I.R.A are the Ultimate Guerilla Fighting Force on the planet but they have no more use…they will be disbanded too!!!

The U.V.F and other Protestant Guerilla Fighters will not be disbanded lol of course they will and if they are so upset by that, that they want to kill…they will be eradicated!!!

The C.I.A are heroes of Con's…his friend Tom Cunningham got him involved with them. He gave Con their reading material for their field agents…a pretty good book lol an exalting book by Steven Pressfield… an English author…called 'Gates of Fire'…it is about the Spartans in ancient Greece…they are the greatest fighters to have graced earth!

The Irish Navy are a bunch of alco's lol so am I…every Irishman loves his grog…the Aussies are the biggest pissheads on the planet…Con will have a house there…to join them in the greatest shindig the world has ever witnessed…the party will be called ConFest!!!

The Kiwi people are a different kind of people than the Aussies… they are funnier…they are very like the Irish because they come from a planet very close to us in the Universe. The Aboriginals are a very wanderlust people…they inspired our King of the Universe Constantine O'Donnell…great ancestor of the index human Donnell to go WALKABOUT…walkabout means to go walking with no direction planned and just encounter what comes your way…it is a Spiritual thing from their world!!!

Crocodile Dundee action hero Paul Hogan was a big influence on Con…he will be able to return to his home in Australia…they wanted too much money off him in taxes the british scum lol…no Irish Pachsion influence there of letting things slide…that means not worrying about it!!!

The people of earth will soon be the happiest people on earth lol it is fun making the smart kids among you laugh!!!

The humans who have not had great schooling will enjoy this book immensely as well...your kids will love you even more if you read extensively on all books available on the planet that look interesting to you...my favourite authors are Tom Clancy...Pachsion man...Stephen King...Britannia man...Irvine Welsh...Britannia man...and of course the favourite of all to him...Andy McNabb...Britannia man...with Pachsion leanings...The SAS man who was captured in the Gulf War... if you decide to read his books...start with Bravo Two Zero...my cousin Moggy who was in the Para's told me this when I joined the Elite Fighting Force of the British...so bloody good at counter terrorism because of their fight with Pachsion lol we taught them a thing or two... Con joined the ranks of the SAS through his cousin James (Moggy) McGilloway...descended from the O'Donnell's as well...he used to read the cartoon comic book for teenagers 'Slaine'...based on a great Celtic Warrior!!!

The movies you should watch are War, Drugs, Mafia, Action, Prison, Thriller, Horror and Romance...do NOT FORGET lots of Comedy as well...'Patch Adams' with Robin Williams is one of Con's most influential movies...it made him go up against the bastard pharmaceuticals who make psychotropic drugs for people who are just a bit down on themselves...the Jews again!!!

The most influential people in the world are Hollywood actors...they will now be getting a Billion dollars a movie and people of all ages will go see their movies all over the planet...there will be Cinemas in every town and city on the planet...it will be your Saturday nights entertainment as a kid...you will see over 18 movies when you are 5 years old...the reading age of this book you are reading...5 years and up...there will be no classification of movies anymore...that was the British people Britannia who brought that in...they are so controlling...their people are so bloody controlling as well...wait till

you read 'Shroove Head'…Con's new book he is writing after this…
also for kids of 5 years and up!!!

The Jewish people that invented psychiatry are going to be vilified in
the history books of humanity…vilified means thought badly of. The
psychiatrists learn medicine first then go after pharmaceutical money…
these are not good humans. They are NOT trying to help the human
race…money orientation…orientation means what drives you…drives
you means what spurs you on…is a Jewish ethos drummed into them
by Zion…ethos means belief!!! Money grabbing Jews…lol.

The planet Zion no longer exists…Britannia blew it up!!!

The Universes people are rejoicing…our parent Universe that controls
all Universes agreed that there should be no evil in the Universe!!!

The Pachsion people are really, really , really advanced but Britannia
have the most vile of weapons…

The people of Britannia are rejoicing as well…the King of Britannia
was executed…that means put to death. The Real English army lol the
Real I.R.A are going to be executed as well…they will be exterminated
like rats…

The I.R.A on Ireland have been fighting the fight against the British
for thousands of years…it is way before history books but we will tell
you all about it in 'Shroove Head'.

The exclamation marks are worrying Con lol…just incase you are as
intelligent as him…you will find that funny!!!

The humour in our language is not as good as English…it is better
but we agreed with the rest of the Universe that English is the most

attractive language lol French is…we agreed that English is the most intelligent language. Prince Harry wouldn't you agree mate?

The English people are really funny…not as funny as the Irish but a close second.

The British people are going to be a funny people without a Royal Family to look up to of their own. They have always had one…ever since their conception…that means thought up of. The last thing that the Letterkenny people of Donegal, Ireland expected was Con to be a Billionaire…they treated him like a poverty stricken nobody…they tried to run him down with cars…they tried to kill him with insults… they are the most evil people in Ireland…stay away from them!!!…We mean that…don't even go there out of curiosity.

America will be loving the aliens new plan…Con will have a commune in California, USA. It will be called Conzion.

New York will be a fabulous place to be in on the 4th of July 2024. The aliens are landing overhead. They will be in orbit above the city and will be visible during the day and night. Don't worry it won't be like the movie where they attack lol.

Con will own the Empire States building and have an apartment on the top floor…he just felt it…he has future sight. His girlfriend Drea Garbula will not be there…of course she will but Con still has his doubts…they are still not talking…they fell out about 7 years ago and haven't spoken since…she is more tempersome than Con ever imagined lol she is just afraid.

The only thing that we are worried about is your parents reading this book faster than you lol they will be asking you what you thought of certain parts?…just tell them to go away and have a wank…a wank is masturbation…this means pleasuring yourself sexually. Girls rub their clitoris…it is located at the top of the vagina like a little bean…Con ex-girlfriend T-Dog used to call it flicking the bean and finger banging lol he loves that one…it makes him chuckle…just rub it gently and you will feel so good…we put it there on humans so they would enjoy sex and sexual pleasure. Men just pull that thing till it explodes…grab it in your fist…wrap your fist around your cock and make the motion of shuffling a deck of cards…this is an old analogy…analogy means likeness…Con just made a valid but funny point…get it hard then chug away!!!

If you want to have a boyfriend then you should know that you must be flirty with them…let them know you are interested in having a sexual relationship with them…all children think about this but up until now it was a tremendous taboo…that means not talked about. Flirting is a game where you say things or do things that will attract a man. Be provocative…that means dirty or sexy…you will have it built into you and know exactly what we mean but there is a little fucking spirit in Con at the minute from the annihilated planet Zion and he keeps interfering with Cons train of thought and he thought you might need to be told what flirty means…we are only too aware that the Jews patronize everybody. If you are a man and you want to attract women then you must be exciting. Con was told this by a very attractive South African woman called Amy Morgan…she was hellbent on riding him lol.

The women that are of the disposition…that means temperament… that means thoughtfulness…then…stay away from them…they are bad news and will get you in trouble…I mean stay the fuck clear of women who try and manipulate. The women you should be interested in are intelligent, funny and good to you. All women do this…we are only joking!!!

All the men that you little girlies should be interested in should not be your father…this is a joke a father is a girls first love…well most of the time…Con just thought of his sister Maggie Moo and thought she did not love her father like that but we can argue vehemently… vehemently means forcefully…that she fancied the hell out of him…he was in her erotic nightmares lol children think it is terrible to have dirty dreams about their parents but they are the closest to them so they will obviously be attracted to them…the Jewish people tried to make this a mental illness…those pesky Jews…their boss man was a fucking idiot called Sigmund Freud…he was a drug addict and a complete fantasist.

The last thing I am going to tell you kids is that sex is the most brilliant delicious thing in the Universe…we are taking out all the taboos… remember what taboo means lol?

The ladies in Cons life were so entertaining…all of them…even the little girls that fancied him because he was sleeping with their mothers lol.

The little boys who fancied him as well used to pester him for blowjobs lol remember what they are…?

Women everywhere will want to sleep with your King Con but he will tell them no sluts allowed…of course he will have relations with them…he is going to have hundreds of children…

This is the new dawn children…what you are reading has been in the pipeline for an eternity…this doesn't seem that long to Con because his mother used to use the word all the time…she was so highfalutin… this means pompous or pretentious lol we are just kidding…she is very intelligent!!!

The millions of years that we have waited to tell you children this information has been the most exciting of our history…so fucking boring lol…we have been waiting for an eternity lol…that's the type of thing she used to say…this book will appeal to her and not affect her blood pressure…Con just thought that we might cure it and we will!!! Then she can read his high-octane account of his life in iCon Wildman101…she won't read it at the minute incase she dies lol.

Cons Granny bust out laughing when we wrote that…Con was her little heathen…that means he did not believe in religion of any sort… fuck the jewish race…they are using psychics to interfere with Cons writing of this book.

Cons Granny O'Donnell was extremely intelligent as well. She was born a Ward…she was from Glasgow in Scotland and Cons Grandpa Charlie swept her off her feet and kidnapped her with loving arms and took her back to Carrowtrasna to live like a poor mans Queen lol they were the Gentry…that means they were the fucking bosses!!!

The I.R.A are not terrorists…they are a reactionary force put together because the British invaded Ireland. The British media portray them as evil because they are evil themselves.

The U.V.F are terrorists. All the paramilitaries of the Protestant side were terrorists. They worked with the British government to stop Ireland becoming a single country again. The British struck a deal with one of our I.R.A heroes, Michael Collins…you will read about him in the future in school…to divide the country into 26 counties in the Republic of Ireland and 6 counties in Britain. This angered I.R.A leaders so they shot him…I do not agree with it…he was in a terrible position and had to make peace for his country so he took their offer and they had peace in the 26 counties. The 6 counties went clean crazy in the last couple of decades lol no they didn't they went complete bananas for 30 years or more until the governments struck a peace deal and the I.R.A hid their weapons lol.

Soyboy is a term that is used for men who are watery and weak…the spirit that is in Cons mind reminds him of this term lol he just thought of it and the spirit left him angrily…Con can see the spirit enter and leave his body…he has tremendous gifts…He is the KING OF THE UNIVERSE!!!

His Universe consisted of Moville for quite a number of years…it is in Donegal. It is what his father would say "A WART ON THE BOLLOCKS OF TIME!!!" The Moville people hated Con when he was growing up. They thought he was spoiled because he was wealthy. He was the least spoiled boy in the area. He got all the toys he wanted but he never really wanted any…he used to play in nature…climbing shit lol.

Moville is another town that we are telling you DO NOT GO NEAR!!! It is so jealous of Con…Con is laughing to himself because they are all buying his book iCon Wildman 101 because their town is mentioned in it and The Giant's Causeway when it comes out in a few weeks time of writing this. Lots of places in Ireland are mentioned in iCon wildman101 and they will probably do the same thing and buy it when it becomes famous in a year from now but they are not as evil as Moville. Con had the most terrible relationship of his life with a little slut of a woman there…she was called Fiona McHenry…their family are descended of the British.

Moville will never be home for his people in the earth. They will all avoid it. The pubs are terrible and have no experience behind the bar… no craic!!!

The people that live there inspired Cons poetry book title 'Anonymous in the town that talks'. They fucking ruin everybody's lives with malicious gossip. They all do it. They are the most evil of people.

They bullied Con forever and they are now paying the price! No more tourism for that little buttfuck town.

RATHMULLAN is going to be infested with locusts on the beach of RATHMULLAN everyday when I am GOD…when I put the book down this time kids to have a spiritual smoke of a cigarette the Universe told me that I was now God!!! So RATHMULLAN you are fucked in the head if you think you can abuse me for these last few years since I moved here to get away from the diseased mentality of Letterkenny or as my beautiful cousin on my mothers side Kristian Capulet Shortt the rapper…Google him…great fucking craic…really funny guy…it runs in the both sides of the Family…calls it Letterfanny lol. DO NOT COME HERE CHILDREN.

RATHMULLAN PEOPLE are Mongoloids.

Derry city is a nice place to drink in lol is it fuck!!!

Londonderry as I will call it forever now is going to lose all their tourism as well…do not go it either…you will get raped and shot!!!

Londonderry is the worst place on earth to have friends in…they all tout on you…this means they grass you up…tell tales kids.

Londonderry is a terrible place because they bullied me as well. They used to taunt me so I would react and then they could tell the police on me and get me locked up in a mental asylum forever.

Belfast is a much nicer city. You will have such an interesting time there. Watch the movie 'Titanic'…it was built there…the Titanic museum is awesome.

The Falls Road is a great place to go drinking…so much colour and craic with the people.

The Shankill Road is fun as well. They have a great sense of humour.

Dublin City is the best place in Ireland for drinking and having the craic. Lots of little pubs and hotels to have a nice fun filled drink in.

Galway City is so musical…I had so much fun there…it is so cosmopolitan. Cultures from all over the world live there. Great bloody craic!!!

Cork City is my second home in Ireland. I was able to express my love for the I.R.A down there. The Jazz festival during the summer is the best time of year to visit…go there and visit the pub the High Bee bar…and the Old Oak.

The only thing that I have left to say about my little country is shag every thing you see!!!

The last thing that I told you was to "Shag"…that means to have sex with…there are lots of aphorisms…this means many names…for sex. They call it BAGGING OFF in the Merchant Navy where Con had a brilliant time bagging off lol.

Drugs are so much fun kids but you will only be doing those when you are 13…this is a lucky number for Con and his Daddy…Con put money on a Roulette wheel one time in an all night Casino in Dublin and won a couple of thousand euro lol he only won 50 euro but it was enough to buy him a few liveners…liveners are what Sailors call alcoholic drinks in the morning…they liven you up!!!

The only thing that excites Con about us taking over is legalising Drugs.

Con has no addictions.

Addictions are a state of mind. You have will power in you…fight children!!!

Alcohol is Cons favourite drug. Next is Marijuana…Google it…then is Ecstacy…then Cocaine and Acid…he has never injected Heroin because his dead Aunt Cathy warned him it was dangerous but he will try it in a safe environment…it always intrigued him because his favourite band when he was young done it…Guns 'N' Roses…YouTube Mr.Brownstone…it is about being hooked on Heroin.

Oasis are Cons favourite band. He loves their lyrics. Noel is an absolute Genius. Liam is so cool that he just exudes it…it makes Con prideful that he is Pachsion. He swells up in the chest when he thinks of Liam… Liam's voice has such a bloody brilliant sound!!!

Robbie Williams is singing at Cons wedding. He will sing one song… Angels. He is Cons favourite singer.

Rod Stewart the Scottish diehard Celtic football club fan…which I support too…is going to sing at Cons wedding as well…he will sing First cut is the deepest.

RATHMULLAN PEOPLE…THE MONGOLOIDS…ARE STILL FUCKING MOUTHING OFF OUTSIDE MY WINDOW…THEY ARE HEARING EVERYTHING I WRITE AND THINK…THEY ARE BEING TOLD BY PACHSION NOW LOL PACHSION ARE TAKING THE PISS OUT OF THEM…WINDING THEM UP… THAT MEANS ANNOYING THEM SO THEY GET ANGRY… TRY IT OUT ON PEOPLE…IT IS GREAT CRAIC…THE MONGOLOIDS ARE TRYING TO TELL ME I CAN'T TELL KIDS WHAT I AM WRITING LOL THEY THINK THESE MONGOLOIDS THINK THEY HAVE AN INPUT LOL THEY

DO NOT EVEN HAVE AN INPUT IN THEIR MARRIAGE
AROUND HERE…

The Dublin people welcomed me in to their city 20 years ago and I am
repaying the dept now…the tourism in Dublin is off the hook at the
minute already but wait till you see how much fun Dublin will be when
I take control of this little bloody country…I am buying it.

The latest woman in my life has just entered. The life I have planned is
awesome. She will be a sister to my married wife Andrea aka Drea…aka
means also known as. They will travel and live with me. I will have a
dozen wives and lots of little children. I am going to be the Landlord of
many pubs, clubs and hotels. I will be the wealthiest man in the world…

Andrea Garbula still hasn't answered my question. She has not told
me if she will spend the rest of her life with me? I am anxious because
I do not want to have a girlfriend that she won't get on with…I think
that it will be ok.

I have no money problems at the minute. My father in his wisdom left
me an allowance of 13 thousand euro for the year. I get 200 euro a
week but I am spending it all on publishing these books for the human
race to read.

The Dublin people are going to be ransacked with tourism lol…I
cannot wait until my book The Giant's Causeway is published…it will
be so awesome!!!

The excitement in Con is building with every word we dictate…he
made a joke one time with a young German Sailor on the Yacht he was
working on…the joke was this…He asked him had he ever read Adolf
Hitler's autobiography Mein Kampf…? The German Sailor replied yes

but he said it was very boring…Con replied "Well he was more of a dictator than a writer!!!" Funny, ha?

The latest girlfriend Con has is from Carndonagh…she knows Con's brothers wife Catherine's sister…she said she is a bit snobby…Con's father hated that word and told Con never to use it to describe someone who is wealthy…he never did but thought a lot about the definition…it means affected by wealth…Catherine's sister is not very wealthy…she just has a bad attitude…so Con believes what his new girlfriend says about her…she is fucking snobby lol.

Little brother James ignores all of Con's messages…Con has been messaging him to get his inheritance…money left to him by his dead father…transferred…sent to him. James won't message him back. This is really annoying him…he no longer has someone in his immediate family that he can rely on. His father always messaged him back and answered his calls…James does neither…don't be like this kids…always be on the other end of the line to help family!!!

I am going to have a cigarette now and relax…cigarettes do not give you Cancer…it is the aliens Pachsion who give the Cancer to people… they were thinning out the population. I will not catch Cancer. The aliens have told me this!!! You won't either kids…Cancer is about to be a thing of the past!!! But remember kids, cigarettes cause your lungs not to be as good for exercise…so go easy on them!

The human race is going to be a wonderful thing in the very near future. They will be so joyous and happy…mental illness will be forgotten and America will be free of the Jewish slavery put on everybody.

The world will be free of the Jewish slavery.

The big pharmaceuticals will no longer be making psychotropic medication for something as trivial as anxiety. Masturbation is a great tension release.

Children everywhere will feel so mature after reading this little book.

Parents that let their children read this book will be honoured in the next life and in this one too by their kids.

The law will hate this book lol…they can get fucked!!!

Rape will be frowned upon…the law on rape is so lenient at the moment…this means they take it very easy on people that commit it… we will be giving the death sentence to anybody that commits it.

Murder will also carry the death sentence.

Do not worry kids…there will be no rape or murder in this new world we aliens are creating.

The aliens all love the planet earth. They are coming here on their spaceships and they will be having the time of their lives. Earth was ultimately created as a holiday destination for the rest of the universe.

God is an O'Donnell. He is the first human being as we have explained. He is the ruler of the universe. He has handed over the rule to Con.

The universe will be the funnest place ever when Con is in complete control of the earth. He is looking forward to explaining this to his new open-minded girlfriend.

I am so excited for you children to not have to worry about crime or poverty. I have lived with both and have been stabbed, robbed and also got into many fights. I've always won them…I'm a warrior…the best Celtic Warrior on the planet!!!

Conor MacGregor is a very well-adjusted human being lol don't even know him but he excites me…I think this excitement comes from the fact that he made his dreams come true from nothing…just like yours truly…me!

If you like fighting then you will love to watch the UFC…it is a great way of learning techniques of how to defend yourself.

I am so confident in my new girlfriend that I do not mind her getting drunk all the time…I like to do this too…it is so much fun!!!

My new girlfriend is called Mairead Butler…she doesn't have a nickname like most Carndonagh people.

She has told me she doesn't want to have sex with me…we'll see about that lol.

The people who love reading are going to be in ecstasy with all of these good books to read. We will be so happy when the rest of humanity picks up the books as well. A lot of people don't read at all. It is a great way to entertain yourself.

I have got the most pleasurable cock on me…Mairead is in for a treat when she sucks it!!!

I am going to be entertaining so many women in the world when I am so bloody rich…remember kids I am God!!!

I will have men as well. They are designed to have a cock in them as well. It goes up the shitepipe lol…I will not be embarrassed about having relations with men that I am attracted to…all humans are Bisexual. I created them like this!!!

Andrea Garbula is a gorgeous human being…I am so excited to have her in my path of destiny…you will meet women and men like this as well.

That is all for tonight lol Con wants to burn the midnight oil…that means work at a project late into the night!!!…we are only winding Con up…he is so interested in what we have to say to you!

Time for a cigarette Con lol feel like one yet kids?

This little paragraph is going to blow your tiny little minds kiddies…the world is going to live forever. The planet will have eternal life soon… there will be another sun put in place and the power of the new sun will bring everlasting life like God promised.

The new earth is going to be a wonderful place to live forever…travel, travel, travel children!!!

That is all Con is writing for tonight. He will be up at the craic of dawn lol another one of his women…you can read about her in iCon wildman101 when you are older…nothing much more different in that book than this one but it is more of a story book…just the way Con tells a tale when he is chatting up beautiful women lol!!!

Drink is all finished in the O'Donnell household of Con. He wants to write some more and on a Saturday night kids…he is so dedicated!!

I have spent my whole life chasing women…all because I want one to spend my life with and have lots of shared memories with…so we can talk, laugh and reminisce.

Andrea Garbula is my soulmate and I would want to not be without her on the rest of my journey in this earth life. I have another wife on Pachsion called Gotta and she is the most beautiful woman in the universe. I will be taking Andrea to Pachsion with me when I die… she will be only too happy to come with me…not serious! She will die before me and go there alone…Gotta will be waiting for her.

The truth of earth is what we are going to talk about now for the rest of the evening.

All the planets are watching Con's every move…they hear everything he says here on earth. His friends from years ago will not believe how much he has grown…especially that buck edjit Thomas Cock…he does not have the intelligence of Con's other friends.

All the planets are loving Con writing a children's book.

The planets of the universe are waiting for Andrea to get back to him on an email so he can be the happiest man in the universe!

All lifeforms of this universe are only too aware that Con is the Don.

The Italian Mafia really inspired Con growing up…his father loved them as well and brought Con up like they bring their children up… with a great sense of pride in your family…

The Greek army the Spartans really inspired Con as well…the book The Gates of Fire was so inspiring that it made Con wonder how they lived all those years ago?

The Germans of the Old world were very inspiring for Con as well. He wondered what life would have been like if they won the world war?

The British army inspired Con as well...he wanted them to let his people be all free to live in their own country.

The Polish people are the nicest people to have a drink with...I have a friend called Maciek but he calls himself Magic...he was a Wildman lol!!!

The London people will be pleased to hear that Con has a very close friend called Ditsy Gilbert...read all about him in iCon wildman101.

The Canadian people will love Con like a brother when he marries Andrea.

I have been to America a few times and always had a great time there... the Americans are so confident...Con loves it in them...just like Prince Harry said in his book Spare...the Americans are the coolest people on the planet!!!

The British government are not going to like it but the I.R.A will be legal very soon.

The American government are always listening out for aliens yet with all my publicity on Facebook they have only looked up my LinkedIn account and not even contacted me...strange lol we know they don't want to help him sell the book iCon wildman101...it is too outrageous for them lol.

The British government are holding back the sale of iCon wildman101 as well. It is out on Amazon in the US but not UK...we are laughing at them...we are only having fun at the moment with earth...Con is your ruler and he is so normal...we made him be this way...you will really warm to him...he is just like his ancestors...a real character!

The Irish people are so hateful to him...the are a very begrudging race of people....we are not like this on Pachsion where the Irish come from but because the island is so small, they hate their neighbour doing better than them lol this will all change very soon!

The teachers Con had growing up were so influential in his maturity… they hated him with a passion lol not all of them Miss Polly liked him!!!

Paddy Connell will absolutely love talking to Con and asking him questions about us aliens…he is Con's smartest friend…Miss Polly's son…they were always interested in aliens. They once sent an SOS into space with a torch…I'm sure Paddy remembers it? We saw it and laughed our heads off…lots of kids do things like that but Con's was serious…he is the Saviour of the human race.

Lisa Connell Patricks sister was bullied by their father…she was adopted and did not get the special treatment Paddy got. We watched this and always knew Con was angry at their father.

Miss Polly was a fun character…she loved getting drunk!!! Patrick and Con loved her fun way…

Andrew Connell is a PhD in something or other…he doesn't like Con anymore…he called him boring lol…the first time in Con's life he was ever called boring…we think he was jealous of him…we know he was jealous of him.

Con's friends from Derry…Londonderry. That is all we have to say… they will all know who they are.

The people of Moville, Donegal are the most vicious people to have an argument with…they are going to regret ever treating Con the way they did.

There are so many people who do not like Con…this will all change in the very near future!

The Letterkenny people are already changing their opinion of him… all because he has a new girlfriend from there…cool, huh?

The Rathmullan people are going to regret treating Con so hatefully as well.

I am so happy to have the aliens in my life…I am never bored…my father always said to me there's no such thing as bored…his only friend that will support his belief in aliens Patrick Connell was always bored as a child…he used to complain to his mother…"Mum I'm bored!!!" I always laughed at him doing this and thought of something we could play at.

We love Con's publisher Writers Apex…they are so really, really, really great!

The publisher Con is dealing with is so cool as well…we all love her…

The death star that people wonder do we have does exist. We are a military nation.

The cigarettes are calling Con again…time for a little breather…Be right back lol.

Con thinks we are boring you lol…we know we're not!

The earths planets…we mean the representation of the universe… this means what in the universe is the same on earth…is about to be all one…this will happen in the universe as well. The lifeforms on the planets of the universe are so excited by Con's life…he met a Ukranian a couple of days ago and he could immediately tell he was going to be lifelong friends with him…he's quite attractive too lol food for thought.

Con will have lots of sex in his life…he loves it…he especially loves getting his cock sucked…you females have such an effect on him…

Your parents are in no doubt thinking the same as my publisher that this book is way too advanced for 5 years and up but we are telling you do not worry it will enlighten them…just watch them mature into little adults!

Con's nuts are itchy lol.

The life that Con lives will all be written down.

Con will own lots of Superyachts. He will have an English Captain on his own private 70 metre yacht. His Captain is great fun. He knows Andrea as well.

Superyachts will be the most fun job in the world. We are going to make it so accessible for all gorgeous human beings. They will be the best and the brightest.

The Merchant Navy will be even more accessible…they don't care how you look!

The college in Ireland…the NMCI is so bloody boring…there should be a pub in it!!!

The maritime museum in Greencastle will be the most interesting museum on the planet…it has a planetarium as well. We will be telling the real history of earth in it…all planetariums of the world will be the same as it.

My favourite movie Patch Adams is so fucking inspiring…

The Mafia movies I watched as a child were so gruesome but so entertaining…my father always let me watch them.

The martial arts movies I watched as a child inspired me so much that I just wanted to be like them and kick everybody's ass lol.

I wasn't a big fan of Horror movies…they made me so paranoid.

I am going to be a huge cinema goer again when I have money. I love the movies…I love all movies…I just love getting some popcorn and a drink and some chocolate and sitting down in the dark of the cinema and letting Hollywood entertain me…they are something special over there.

There will be so many movies made of Con's life…there will not be any killing in it but there will be some crazy ass fighting lol.

The movies will be based all around Ireland and wherever in the world he has been.

Colin Farrell the Dub is one of Con's favourite actors…he has not crossed paths with him but when he does, he'll encourage him to go on the beer with him…he won't say no!

Colin Farrell was so good in the movie Alexander that it brought Con to tears…he was watching the movie in his sitting room when his parents were in bed. The movie was so close to his life.

Colin Farrell also appeared in the movie Tigerland…Con was very like his character in it.

The C.I.A movie The Recruit with Colin was a huge inspiration to him.

The movies with Daniel Day Lewis all inspired Con.

There is a lot of entertainment out there for you to enjoy…do not sit and watch mindless crap on the internet…watch a movie or read a book.

The aliens know you are going to be reading this book many times.

They are loving trusting you with the future of the earth…you are the future!

The aliens from the other planets cannot wait to visit their brethren on this planet…Con has made that happen…you will all read how it came about in iCon wildman101…and you will see it has not been easy…

We are loving Con checking how many words he has written…he is so determined to get this book written before Christmas.

Con loves swimming in the sea…he always opens his eyes under the water…his daddy taught him when he was really young to open his eyes and enjoy the underwater.

I am tired now and feel like a wank lol just having a laugh…I'm saving myself for my new girlfriend…she has invited me to her mother's for Christmas! Goodnight little people…

T'is morning time and I'm in the mood for some hanky panky lol know what that means kids? Lol

I'm in a great mood today…I am meeting my girlfriend tomorrow. She will be half cut…that means a little drunk but I don't mind…I'll join her in the party!

I have a little to tell you about the aliens today…the aliens are always going to be part of your lives. They will be issuing orders through me…

they will be telling everybody how to live their lives to the optimum.…. that means the best that it can be.

The aliens want me to reach 20, 000 words today. I'm at 11,000…that is a good chunk of writing!

The aliens are so excited about me meeting a new woman…it's been years since I have had one!

The last girlfriend I had was a psychopath…she was a psychiatric nurse.

The only thing I am worried about meeting Mairead is that she is not really that jealous of me with other women lol I think it's the future!…I know it's the future!!!

The hotel Dillon's are going to be visited tomorrow…they barred me for screaming Tiocfaidh ar la!!!

Tiocfaidh ar la is an I.R.A slogan…it means in Irish OUR DAY WILL COME!!!

I am wondering what else the aliens have to tell you?

The aliens are laughing their heads off…they have so much to tell but I do not know what it is?

The aliens are only having fun with the earthlings right now…they are telling me little snippets of info…there is the whole universe to talk about…have you any questions you can think of?…ask in your head now and your inner voice will answer you…that is your alien Pachsion guide guiding you…listen to it throughout your life and you will always be correct in everything you do…must go clip my nails…it is much easier to type when your nails are neat and tidy!…Done!!! So much easier…

The only thing on earth that Con is afraid of is his fellow countrymen…
they have tried to kill him.

The last thing Con wants to do is get his hole with a slut…he loves
sluts…so did his Dad lol.

I have been all over the planet lol no I haven't I have only been to 35
countries…but I have never hardly paid for it with my own money…
it has always been with work…great way to see the world but I think
backpacking with loads of money in the bank is even better…do that
children…you will have lots of fun and learn the guitar and songs to
sing at the campfire.

Con used to sing in the Gospel choir with his mum…he did not
know all the words and never learned them off…he was just making
everybody in the community like him again…singing in church lol…
he was so badly behaved with alcohol and drugs that everybody in the
community was talking badly about him. It worked and he stopped
singing then with the church choir…they did not exactly have the same
sense of humour as him lol. The only thing that he was annoyed about
with the choir was that there was only one good looking girl in it…she
was extremely pretty but married…as Con's Captain friend Scott says
A RING DOESN'T COVER A HOLE…can you figure that one out
children? Lol.

The last thing Con is going to write before he has his morning glory lol
he won't be getting that for a few weeks yet but he can't wait to ride the
ass off his girlfriend…she has a glorious bum…great for smothering
yourself in and penetrating deep inside…Oooohhh lol.

My cousin Kristian Capulet Shortt is living in the Seychelles in
Africa…he is married there to a gorgeous black woman…she looks so

delightful…I hope he lets me sleep with her lol just kidding! Go and visit him there, children…he will show you his new home.

…my new girlfriend wants to visit him…I think she fancies his ass lol.

My other cousin Azariah…Kristian's sister is friends with Mairead… they like doing ecstasy together. I am taking ecstasy tomorrow…it is a great drug!

The only worry I have with taking ecstasy is that it is so bloody good you just love to take it more and more…it makes you LOVED UP!!! That means it makes you feel like you are in love with people…it makes your brain so alive.

I am going to talk to you now about the universe…Con is getting impatient with us talking as he feels nothing important but we know you are enjoying hearing about his life…aren't you kids?!

The universe is made up of about 500 planets with life on them like earth. The God you pray to is the most fun individual in the universe!

All the planets are really well looked after by God…he makes them so happy but some of them like to have wars and enjoy fighting with one another. We Pachsion people do not like that. That is why the earth was created…to stop all the wars on the planets and have peace throughout the universe. Pachsion is a really fun place to live. It is the oldest of all the planets. God created it first. O'Donnell is the oldest name in the universe. The other people of the other planets have lots of time to be at one with each other when we bring peace to the universe.

The Ocean of earth is like travelling on a SPACESHIP when you are on a ship…try it kids.

The spaceships we have…this is really interesting Con…are absolutely massive. They are the size of Ireland. They can hold millions of people.

The movie INDEPENDENCE DAY about the aliens was very similar to what we can do to other worlds. We will not be doing this to earth… watch it but please do not be frightened…we are very peaceful.

The movie IN THE NAME OF THE FATHER with Daniel Day Lewis is one of Con's favourite I.R.A movies…his other favourite one is the one with Liam Neeson…MICHAEL COLLINS.

The other movie Con really likes is COOL HAND LUKE with Paul Newman…he is the coolest actor to be in prison in Hollywood…watch it and learn how to behave if you ever get into trouble lol…there will be no crime when you are growing up…you will learn about it in school. School is about to be so interesting!

The books that Con reads are given to him by his mother.…she loves fiction and so does Con.

The only thing that we are going to be destroying is the military all over the world…they will no longer be needed. They will get jobs like normal people. The laughter out of the Britannia people when we think this…they are watching now because Con impressed them so much by getting a British Captain for his Superyacht. They know he does not hold any grudges against the British people. He has cousins there who have got the most wicked sense of humour. He loves the British sense of humour…it is very like the Irish one!

The Scottish people are so unlike the rest of Britain…they are not from the same planet as them. They are from Pachsion…we have already told you this but we are making sure you remember.

The Welsh people are a very easy going people. They come from a little planet close to Britannia and they are allies with them in the universe… that is why they are part of Britain on earth. The whole of Britain will now be under the control of us…the Pachsion people. The Pachsion people have won the world war on earth.

The wars that are raging on earth at the moment will all stop immediately when we come to earth and have a massive party.

The only thing that we will not allow is a massive black dick in Con's asshole…he wonders what it would feel like? Lol.

The next thing we would like to tell you about our spaceships is that you will all be allowed to travel on them. You will be visiting other planets.

The life on these planets will be so alien to you. They are so advanced.

The word count is going up quickly.

The other thing Con wants to do to his girlfriend of 1 week is give her a massive orgasm.

The men of earth at the minute do not pay enough attention to the female orgasm. They will learn how to control their ejaculation like Con can. He can make himself last for hours without cuming.

The parents of the children who allow their kids to read this book will be so involved with their children's evolution.

The American kids will love being the coolest kids on the planet.

Con loves their sports.

The Norwegians are pretty cool as well. Con has an ex-girlfriend living there…she still loves him! She gives the best blowjobs on the planet. She swallows the spunk. Con absolutely loves women doing this…a German woman did this for him in Mallorca as well. She was a real cool girl!

The only thing Moville people like to hear is a Moville person doing well…sometimes not even then!

Con is from Carrowtrasna…Google maps it! Con's house is right beside the Drunken Duck bar…the bar he grew up in…that was great fun for him! A Carndonagh man that owned the Sportsman's Inn was their first customer. Con got him to sign the visitors book…he had a condom in his wallet and he showed them…their father was out at the time. They hadn't even poured a pint for anybody…the people of Carndonagh are very nice people.

The Greencastle people are very nice people as well. Lot's of them come from a fishing background. Con done fishing as well. He couldn't wait to get away from working in the bar…he was so fed up with working in it every day!

Con's mother and father were paying him and his sister 1 pound an hour but they were working so many hours that their parents decided they were giving them too much money so they decided to give them 50 quid a week lol. As Con said in an interview for the Irish Air Corps when he was 17…my parents paid me weekly…very weakly lol!

The Irish Air Corps for Con was a stepping stone to becoming an Astronaut. He wanted to go into space and now his dreams are going to come true. The aliens love his adventurous side. He loves to go walkabout.

The Irish Army was also on the cards for Con to join…he had not heard of the Irish Rangers wing or he would have definitely joined.

The money to work in the Irish Army was not enough to entice him… that means encourage him.

Con did not know what he wanted to do when he decided he could not be an Astronaut. He really liked Engineering and was at the top of his class in it. He did not know which type of Engineering he would like to do so he decided against it. He eventually done Electronic engineering and kind of enjoyed it…he thought he might be a bomb expert lol.

Con found his love in the working life when he went away to sea. His Daddy told him FIND A JOB YOU LIKE AND YOU'LL NEVER WORK AGAIN!!! This is what he done. He loved waking up in the morning and already being at work! He loved the time off as well. When he was working…he was working but when he was off, he could party like crazy lol.

The pub was so informative…that means educational…for him growing up. There was so many intelligent people drinking in his fathers pub. They used to tell him things and educate him of the world. So much interesting things happened him when he was working there.

The aliens are going to help Con open up the Drunken Duck again. You will be able to visit it and sign the visitor's book!

We are so fucking interested in the life you will all lead after reading this book…we know it will inspire you all…time for a cigarette for Con!

We are so happy!!! Con just put on a wash for the first time in weeks!

This girlfriend is really having an effect on him lol…she isn't answering either…must be still drunk!

The aliens have got so much to tell you young kiddies…the world is so much fun when you get older.

The last thing Con must have before he visits his girlfriend is a masturbatory experience lol no, he won't. He will use his charm and get his wicked way with her!

That is all we have to say about the bullshit that you must have a wank before you meet a new girl…it was in a movie called There's something about Mary…Cameron Diaz is really cool in it…Con wants to be her fuckbuddy…every time he is in L.A they will meet up and make passionate love!

Con has lots of women he wants to have luscious love with…Jennifer Aniston is another one…she is the most attractive woman in Hollywood… apart from Angelina Jolie…that woman really turns Con on!!!

Brad Pitt is a really cool guy but he gets all the women so Con doesn't really like him lol he wants to have a drink with him and smoke some weed and do some Cocaine with him…they will be best buddys.

There are lots of actors that Con wants to be friends with…singers as well. Bono from U2 is one man that Con would love to go on the drink with…they call it going on the beer but you could be drinking anything!

We are reaching 14,000 words and it is really simple…Con will write 30,000 words today and have the book nearly finished.

Larry Kealey from Greencastle lied to the powers that be when Con's father was losing his job.

The people from Shrove have always for a hundred years been the Pilots…that means they drove the ships up and down the river Foyle to Londonderry…Derry for you staunch people lol.

Danny McCann was a bit of an idol for Con when he was a teenager. Danny had a wicked appetite for female company. Con admired how he got the women.

Con's cousin Mick Cavanagh also had a good way about him...he was always drinking and driving...he crashed 17 cars drunk at the wheel lol and never ever hurt himself...he was so lucky. He has a pub in Moville but it is not that much fun because he told Con to be quiet and not be excited when he is drinking in it...not much fun! Maybe he will change his mind when he reads this...Con hopes so...he loves his cousin.

The only thing that Con can think of when he thinks of Mick is "What is blue and doesn't fit?"..."A dead epileptic!!!" Con's cousin Paul that died is Micks younger brother and he just told him to put that joke in... he was epileptic...he said Mick is going to kill him and then laughed and left to go back to Pachsion.

Sally and Charlie...Micks mother and father are really nice people... they never believed I was mentally ill or did nearly all my relatives. My father was so cruel on me...he forced me to take awful medication that leaves you so stupid...he said DEPRESSED IS GOOD!!! Then he laughed at his own joke...I felt like ripping his heart out...the aliens did this for me years later.

The worry has set into Con's head that his new girlfriend has stopped talking to him...it is normal at the start of a new relationship to have these worries...he is not immune to these thoughts...even as the King of the Universe lol...imagine? Lol.

Con will not worry if she doesn't turn up...he will have a few drinks and smoke some weed with his new Ukranian friend...he is a good looking man...maybe he will give Con a blowjob...you never know!!!

That turned Con on!!!

Well a little bit…he adores women.

The Bisexual side of Con is only in its infancy…that means he is only waking up to it…

The real people who like Con will have lots of time for him when he is drinking around Letterkenny.

The only thing that Con really loves is sex with women…he does not get really aroused by men…this will not change in his life!!!

The only reason that aliens are writing this book is to evolve you into aliens yourselves. You are all aliens…God made you that way!!!

God is not coming to earth…he has handed the universe over to Con… the aliens are laughing…Con jumped the gun a bit there…God handed the universe over to us the Pachsion people and we are to guide Con on what to do with earth…so Con is God on earth!!!

The last thing we want you to think is that we are preaching…we do not preach.

Con's girlfriend just messaged him…Phew! Lol. She is hungover…you will learn what this is when you reach 7…

The fun Con will have tomorrow is setting in…he is so excited!!!

We'll tell you all about it…this is the start of Con's reign over the universe.

Con's new girlfriend stood him up…back to Andrea lol.

Con's new boyfriend is only a friend…he is not liking our thoughts on him having sexual relations with men.

Arsenio said to Con "no gay shit". Lol he was only joking with him!!!

Britannia has crumbled. Pachsion are the rulers of the universe.

You young kids are reading what is happening in the universe and earth as it happens live with Con.

All of the worlds that are on earth are now listening to Pachsion guides. All inner voices of the universes people are listening to the rulers of the universe.

The only thing Con has to worry about is running out of money to publish and market his books…he will write one more book after this one…then everything will be on a blog…a blog children is an online autobiographical account of life and living.

The British people will not really like being told what to do by an Irish God but that is how it's going to be!!!

Pachsion is full of joy today….the music singer Shane MacGowan has reached the gates of our world. He did it sober…a first for him lol… he can get as drunk as he wants now!!!

The only people Con O'Donnell fears in this world are the Real I.R.A. They continuously threaten him everyday outside his window and they are so evil that they do not care that he is helping the world out.

Con is not really afraid of anybody in the entire universe.

Apart from his vicious mother…she is a scary individual.

All parents have a scare tactic with their children. This will never change until you reach the ripe old age of 15 and receive your millions of dollars to proceed with your life.

The wondering of Con is getting funny…he is wondering what we have left to say to you? We have told you so much but it just dawned on him that there are so many other cultures at war with one another. There is volumes and millions of volumes to read about the earth and universe!

Germany is a culture that had world domination in its mind.

Con has a German girlfriend. She is beautiful but nearly too old to have kids. Her brother is a lawyer and Con figured out that he needed Con to get his wicked way with his sister if the world was about to change for the better!

The last thing for 1 hour until Con gets a little inebriated…that means drunk kids…is to let you all know that you will excel at school after reading this book.

That was an enjoyable hour…I received an email from the best publisher on the planet telling me that I can put the new blurb on The Giant's Causeway book about Andrea. I also watched a Robbie Williams anecdote on the Graham Norton show…it was hilarious.

Robbie Williams is without doubt my favourite singer.

I have so much to tell you children.

My life is running parallel to Robbie Williams.

I am the wildest alien on planet earth!!!

I am the only alien that the aliens Pachsion talk to. Con thought they were talking to his soon to be wife Andrea Garbula…we've been away from the keyboard awhile…just getting acquainted again with my wife! We were not talking to her. We were bullshitting Con in his mind…he could hear Andrea talking about him…he has been emailing her for the last 3 months lol weeks and she will not return his wanton lustful advances lol he's just trying to reconnect after 7 years…a bit long to be away from the one you love!!!

I am a little heartbroken…Gotta…my wife on Pachsion is guiding Andrea in her thoughts and daily life…Andrea used to be a Chief Stewardess on Superyachts but evolved into a Chef…it was Con that told her it was a good career move because she would be able to retire from Superyachts with Chefing and possibly open a restaurant… they are now going to open a chain of high end Superyachting style restaurants all over the world…they are going to be called Andrea O'Donnell Masturchef.

The love that I have is so unique. I designed Andrea to be my wife…I am God!!!…that is why she loves getting her drink on lol!

I have a joke for you…a woman said to the man "You smell nice…what have you on?" The man replies "Thank you…I've a hardon but I don't think you could smell it!!!"

The only thing I love more than Andrea is crack cocaine lol she hates the stuff…probably just as well…I fucking love all drugs…I love to get whacked out of my head…that'll probably change when I have kids…I think so anyway! Lol.

Andrea is a hot topic for me…I am so in love with her family history as well. Her Grandfather was very intelligent…that I think is where she gets it from…I don't really know that for sure…I haven't met her father yet.

Her little brother gave me the biggest boost ever…I told him a few years back on facebook that I should have asked Andrea aka Drea to marry me…he said "Perhaps!" It was enough encouragement for me to get my life together and get as fucking filthy rich as I could and win her heart!!!

The mental health in my life is over and done!

You kids are going to be the healthiest mentally sound kids on the planet with all this information in those beautiful little heads of yours.

I love talking to children…it reminds me of bringing up my little brother…he listened to everything I said. He is so intelligent. He does not really listen anymore. He is a bit…well a lot independent. I'm very proud of him.

His wife Catherine is a school teacher…a bit of a bad girl lol I like it in her…I picked the AC/DC rock song Thunderstruck for them to walk to the top table when they got married. I thought it was very fitting. They both pretend they're goody two shoes but they both love to drink and get rotten drunk lol.

Prince Harry is not as bad a man as everybody makes out. He misses his mother everyday…a bit fucking much at his age if you ask me…you get over that shit pretty quick.

My mother is now talking to me. She wasn't for a few months. I threatened to kill her on our family O'Donnell group chat on WhatsApp lol…I was setting her up! I was proving a point. She told my family that she had no input in whether I was locked up in the asylum or not. As soon as I threatened her she called the asylum and had me locked up again. I was only out a few days when I done it. She was a complete bloody cunt…it was hilarious! I picked up all the women in there. The Doctor went bananas and injected me with medication that stops your sex drive…it did nothing but stop my erection and ejaculation… ejaculation is where sperm comes out of your penis. It is for making babies. The sperm fertilizes the female egg and a baby is formed. It did not shut me up tho lol…fucking evil sadistic cunts!!!

The only people that care about me are on the family WhatsApp group chat O'Donnell and of course my publisher and her publishing team. I have been through hell!!!

My publisher head hunted me from another company…it's a great little story…I'll tell it in interviews!

I have the most wicked sense of humour and justice…it always involves laughing!

The people that do not behave well sexually around kids will have their genitals amputated…that includes the women!!!

I have only scratched the surface with writing my life story. It is so long and so fucking boring lol one international incident after another motherfucker!!!

The Superyachts I worked on always had femme fatales…I nearly always fell in love with them. They were always so dead on and absolutely stunning…a real turn on for me…even with Andrea on the scene lol. I once had a photo shoot on a yacht with a beautiful Stewardess that fancied the pants off me. We were taking photos to send Andrea lol the Stew was ripping but I was the Superior Officer and she wanted to fuck me lol.

The last thing I want to be is a male slut lol too fucking late…my son will be the same…I'm the same as my Da…lol.

I have always been a ladies man…ever since I was a little boy. When I was 5 the girls in my class asked me to see my penis…they were all turned on…I took it out and showed them…they were all laughing and excited. I could see it in their eyes.

My favourite thing to do to a woman is be exciting. Every woman alive ever on planet earth enjoys an exciting man…be the excitement in their life and you will always be happy.

My Andrea has yet to experience real excitement with me. She has only heard about exciting times I have been through…I have been through so many of them!!

I am off the cigarettes because Andrea bloody hates them. She thinks they are disgusting. I'm inclined to agree. Do not smoke kids. They are poison.

I am going to put my head down now and continue in the morning.

Goood morning kiddleys lol that reminds me of a joke my cousin Styley told me years ago…it goes like this…a man walks into the butchers and asks the butcher for a pound of kiddleys please…the butcher looks at him quizzically and says don't you mean kidneys sir?…the man said that's what I said diddle I?

I'm in the mood for a game of my favourite pastime in the Universe… Pool!

The I.R.A are my homepeople…they come from Pachsion. They have gone rogue. They are my army. They annihilated the Brits. They are now to be dismantled.

Sinn Fein the political wing of the I.R.A are nothing but retarded kids with a feeling of absolute power. They wield that power over anybody they think is weaker than them…they are fucking bullies…they have been trying to make me kill one of them (so they could be martyred!) for gaslighting and insulting me for 20 years. They have been accosting me in shops, pubs and on the street all over Ireland. It will not stop until they all realize they are living in the pearl of danger. The aliens Pachsion are going to give every last one of them Cancer of some sort. That'll sort the cunts out!!!

I do not really give a damn about nationality all over the world. I treat people as I find them. This is a great way to be kids. If people are nice and genuine to you…then you reciprocate…reciprocate means return the feeling.

The very last thing I am going to be is a tyrant. My father was a tyrant and so is my mother. They both have very big egos. I do not even have an inkling of an ego. You should not either. Women will love you even more for it if you do not bum and blow…bum and blow is a Londonderry saying…it means boasting…telling people how great you are!

The I.R.A are serious bummers and blowers. You'd swear they'd won the Universe the way they carry themselves. Not all of them but the little fucking foot soldiers with massive egos on them. They are the kind of people that get you in trouble!

The u.v.f are really annoyed at the I.R.A for winning the war against the Britain they adopted as their ruler…fucking idiots!!!

The other paramilitaries that are governed by the British Crown have all been disbanded forever. They will not be selling drugs either…the drugs that are all going to be legal will be sold in shops where you can buy milk and bread. It will be so normal.

The drug barons of Columbia are going to be the richest people on the planet.

The D.E.A…drug enforcement agency will disband as well.

The F.B.I will not have any crimes to solve after we aliens arrive next Christmas day. The crime on earth will all cease! They will also disband. The employees will take up counselling as will all military personnel from all over the world…those people have serious drive and ambition in the them. They will instil their beliefs and gumption into civilians all over the world. It will be a highly rewarding job with major benefits like good pay and great holidays…and a massive early pension.

Mental health is going to be eradicated off the face of the planet. The psychiatrists that Con hates so much because of their evilness and manipulative cuntish ways will not be practicing medicine or counselling if that is their background. They will all be going to a plantation in Australia. It will have only water and the bare essentials for surviving for a few years…they will all die of starvation. That is all psychiatrists and psychiatric nurses. From all over the world!!! This is the punishment for killing and destroying so many people!!

Dr. Haley is a fucking imbecile.

I am wondering is this little bit of info on the last few paragraphs a little too advanced for you kids? Lol you'll be fine…

The only thing Con has in his mind writing this book is hitting the target of 30,000 words. We think it's hilarious!!! Considering he is writing the world as it is and how it is going to be!!

The women who are in love with our King Con will not be saddened by his upcoming marriage to the Bombardier girl Andrea Garbula. They will be happy for him. There is a lot of them in the world lol.

The last thing before Con takes a little breather and lies back with his feet up for half an hour because it is still early in the morning and his brain hasn't quite woken up yet is the wank of a lifetime happened thinking about shagging his wife in the shower after they had anal sex and she shit all over him…Andrea you filthy bitch lol.

The life as a poet is so exciting…one of my Stewardess lovers said after I professed my undying love for her that she wasn't surprised at the depth of my love…she said poets feel life the most…bright woman! This poem about Andrea is a little short period…hopefully she'll still be getting hers when we marry. I want to have lots of children with her…

Andrea…

My love is unfounded,
In a world full of pain,
Where everything is hurtful,
And there is nothing to gain,
The wonderful joy,
You give my life,
Will be so riveting,
With you as my wife…

The Bombardier name really tweaked my interest in Andrea at the beginning…I knew right away she was wealthy. I always want my woman to come from wealthy backgrounds. They do not always but I never waste my time on these women. You should do the same children. The upbringing of wealthy people is far more superior to poor people. There is no apology coming to the poor people reading this book. I do not think there will be many anyway. They do not have the capability of realising there is an evolution going on. They are buried into their cheap Android phone and talking about inane crap on the social media about celebrities. I do not give one flying fuck if there is a hate campaign against me for saying this because you do not have to think like a poor person just because you have very little money…I have proven this. I come from a relatively well off background and had a wonderful upbringing…I've been in and out of so much trouble that my cash flow has not always been solid enough to bring me great wealth…up until now…I am a bloody poor person. But I do not think like one. I be like a wealthy Billionaire and believe I can change the world. The begrudging that is omnipresent in the lower classes is going to be stamped out. There will be no more jealousy. Money will be allocated to all people of the world but there will always be those with more wealth than others. They were either left it or worked for it. The lower class people nearly always complain about the more fortunate. Stop fucking doing it. You're embarrassing yourself…making your children bitter…and ultimately being so ignorant that your personal wealth will never be enough to make you happy!!!

The Bombardier family will soon be my family. I look forward to having nights out with them. Andrea said they're great fun!!!

The Garbula family weren't talked about…I'm sure they are fun as well.

The O'Donnell family all love their drink and drugs…well most of them. They love a good shindig…whether it's a funeral or wedding lol.

I am fast approaching 20,000 words. Exciting for me to get this magnificent book written and into the history books of Earth.

The only thought in Con's head is to ly down again. Listening to us talking to him for the last 3 years constantly is now wearing him down.

It will not continue much longer. Andrea will take over from us. She will constantly talk lol. Con will not get tired of her chitter chatter. Her accent is so attractive. She sounds like a movie star to Con.

The battery is running out and Con doesn't want to get off his fat ass and plug in the laptop…he is right beside it lol fucking do not be like this kids. Con is behaving so like the people he really despises…lazy fat stupid humans. Now he has his drive back!!! He's doing it now…

The people that Con does not like are going to be exterminated. They will be killed with terminal diseases. Con's mother was such a cunt to his father and his family that we gave her Cancer…his father was so upset that we spared her. Con was not really worried.

The little people that get upset at what Con is writing can go and fuck their mothers!!!

I am I.R.A.

I am SAS.

I am C.I.A.

The Special Forces are in my thinking as well. I am Irish Ranger Wing.

Kids there will be none of these groups of people when you get older. They are finished on earth. Us aliens are bringing world peace.

The only thing that Con could think about when we said world peace there was his favourite alcoholic singer Shane MacGowan saying on his death bed to his wife Victoria who always caught Con's eye because she is a white witch…that he wanted world peace!!!

The other thing he done that Con thought was quite cool was put 10,000 euro behind his local bar in Tipperary, Ireland for the locals to drink…Con will do something similar in Antibes!!!

Con and Andrea and kids will live in Antibes in the South of France. Their children will go to local primary schools until they are 10 then they will go to boarding school…they will love the adventure of being away from home and get into so much mischief lol.

The Cap D'antibes is Con and Andrea's new home in the South of France. They love France and Andrea is French Canadian. So attractive in Con's head…and loin lol.

Andreas mother has been asked by us to give Con and Andrea a private jet with a crew for life from the Bombardier riches. We know this will happen. They will all decide that it is a wonderful gift. Con just said in his head don't forget for them to cover the fuel as well lol. Her uncle made a joke that he will paint it pink. They have a great sense of humour!!!

Con's friends that disowned him are going to be spitting blood when they hear about him and Andrea on all the media channels and all over the social media and internet everyday for the rest of their lives…You have no idea how famous Con and his wife are going to be!!!

The publishing company Writers Apex are going to have worldwide acclaim for their treatment of an alien. They will be the biggest self-publish company in the world!

Con's publisher is getting 1 billion dollars from us for being so good to our King Con.

I have so many good pictures for the cover photo of my front covers of my books. The books will be so famous everywhere…

I have so many good friends…they are all over the world.

I can be so obnoxious lol never in my life have I been obnoxious…I will be the best rich person on the planet and in the Universe. Andrea already is a beautiful rich woman…I do not want to be a beautiful rich woman lol I want to be a handsome rich man with new Hollywood smile teeth!!! And of course thin as well…the aliens have told me I will be down to 11.5 stone in 6 months time. They are going to help me.

The children of my loins and Andreas loins JESOS does that make my motor purr lol are going to be so fun, smart and attractive. I'll probably want to ride them myself lol.

I have so much respect for Donald Trump lol I used to but he made such a fuck up of being the President of America I lost all respect for him…especially bringing in no abortion. You should be able to choose if you want to have a child or not.

God does not care about human life…I think people who are dying must have figured that one out with all their unanswered prayers lol Con is giggling…he is so fucking evil!!!

Children have lots of flings when you are growing up and also in adulthood. Get as much experience of love and eroticism as you can… it will make you so happy in your life…Con is a complete sex addict… Con's father made a joke when Con was in the mental asylum for the first time. The man in the next bed from Con was down on the ground prostrating…that means he was making the sign of the cross with his arms and body and praying to God. I told Dad that he was a religious addict. Dad said why doesn't he get addicted to something good like sex? It made me laugh.

Dad was so funny sometimes. He really had some great one liners. I told him about my connection with the Chinese Triads and he said it sounds like Criminal dot org. It was a location joke…you had to be there.

My Dad read my first manuscript of iCon…my autobiography. He said after he had read it I should have called it 40 shades of green… making a joke about 50 shades of grey. He was so happy I got laid so many times lol.

My mother will not even read anything in the book…she is not a very good example of how to be a leader's mum.

I think and know this book will be read from cover to cover in one day. Kids you will all be talking about it at school and with your brothers, sisters and friends.

Adults that read this will be very informed afterwards. They will get more out of it than the kids.

Con is duking at the word count. He just wants to lie on the couch and think of Andrea…Awww!!!

Con is going on the be a Captain Unlimited…that is the biggest certificate you can achieve at Nautical college.

Con's kids will all be going to work on ships as well. He thinks some of them will like the Merchant Navy and others will like Superyachting. We can tell him they will all want Superyachting. Captains and Stewardesses. Probably Chefs as well like their mom.

Con just thought I'd like my children to call me Dad and their mother mom…they will probably have a transatlantic accent…a mixture of Canadian and Ireland. Pretty cool mix if you ask us!!

Con's in laws will love him to bits. He loves their little Andrea so bloody much. He is going to change the world for her!!!

He was going to do it anyway but why spoil the story with the truth lol old Donegal saying!!!

The Gardai Siochana are on a publicity surge trying to cur favour with the public that they are so cool!!! It is going to explode in their faces when Con takes charge of the world. All cops will be disbanded. They will not fucking be counsellors. The last thing we aliens want is their belligerent attitude prevalent amongst the Irish people en mass.

The President of Ireland will soon be a UFC fighter. Conor MacGregor. He will be a bit of life compared to the little penguin.

Con is Batman from Gotham city in the comic books…he is one of Con's heroes for fighting crime…real bad crime…not Con crime… lots of fun.

Con is Spiderman as well. That is what the Sint Maarten people called him because he jumped through a raging flaming hot fire at a beach bar party in the island of Sint Maarten.

Con is Superman. He will be able to fly in a few years time.

Con is so gullible sometimes!!!

Don't be gullible kids…gullible means believing what you are told without questioning if it could be untrue…Con is the least gullible human on the face of the earth…he grew up in a pub in Ireland with lots of adults trying to take the piss out of him…they never ever succeeded.

Con is getting excited at the word count!

We are finishing the book here!...only joking around with Con lol you should have seen the panicked look on his face. He wants lots more information in it. We are just finishing for the day!

LOL THAT'S ALL FOLKS!!! GO IN PEACE TO LOVE AND BE LOVED BY YOUR FELLOW HUMAN BEING...BOOK FINISHED!!! Con is now relieved...funny as fuck!

www.ingramcontent.com/pod-product-compliance
Lightning Source LLC
Chambersburg PA
CBHW030438120726
47903CB00003B/1024